Hello everyone at
Casorso Elementary!

Keep reading and playing outside!

For Kyla and Lincoln with so much love ~ D.A.

Watch for these icons in the story - see back cover for more details

Resourceful

Peaceful

Considerate

Ethical

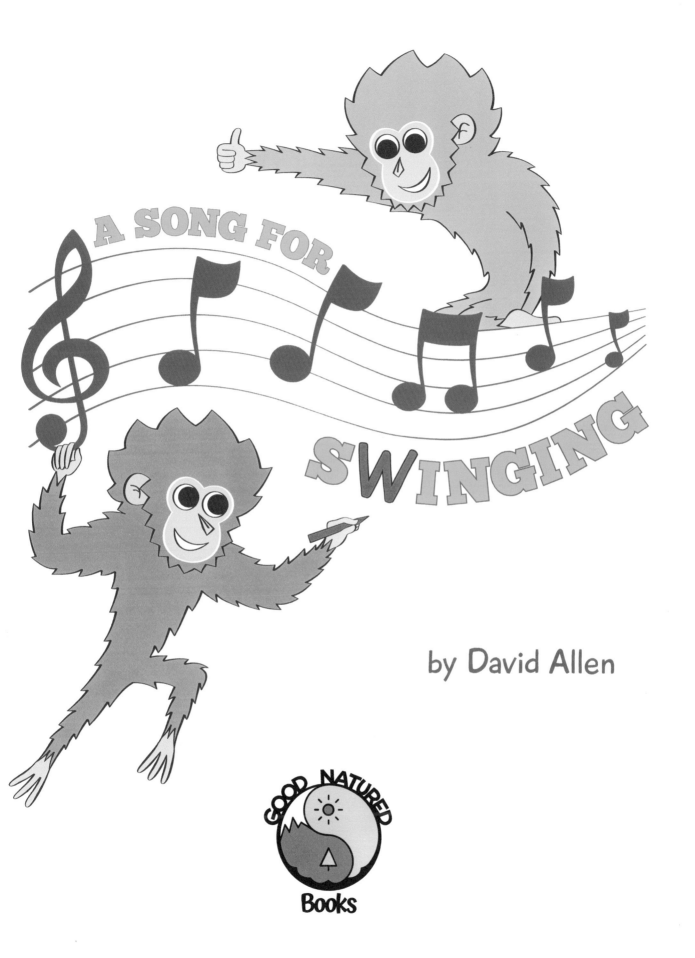

A SONG FOR SWINGING

by David Allen

GOOD NATURED Books

Outside in the forest
above the big trees,

two little gibbons
played in the breeze.

Tingle was swinging
on branches up high.

Tangle was jumping in leaves from the sky.

They had fun in nature
and loved everything.

To all of their friends,
the gibbons would sing!

Then Tingle worked hard
to climb to the top.

She saw a nice mango
that happened to drop.

At first she was sad
as it went to the ground,

but then she was glad -
there were more to be found!

Tangle saw something
while swinging on through.

He caught it, then thought about what he should do.

Although he was hungry
and would have liked some,

he took back the fruit
to where it came from.

Tingle said, "Thank You,"
but did not need another...

and offered her own
as a gift to her brother.

Now Tangle had both
which did not seem fair,

so he broke them in half
because they could share.

They had a great snack
as the sun went to bed,

then the forest all sang
to the gibbons instead.

FUN FACTS ABOUT GIBBONS!

 While gibbons may look like monkeys, they are actually apes. Did you see that they do not have a tail?

 Gibbons spend almost all of their time in trees, swinging and leaping from branch to branch. They have strong arms and can swing very quickly - sometimes even faster than a car!

 They live in the dense forests of Southeast Asia, as well as parts of India and China. Try finding these places on a map!

 Gibbons mostly eat different kinds of fruit. Did you notice the one that Tingle found in the story? It is called a dragon fruit and is very healthy and delicious!

 Gibbons hardly ever touch the ground and do not make nests or homes. They sleep by just sitting on a strong branch!

 Gibbons really do sing! They make high and low sounds in a way like people can. Gibbons will sing by themselves or with others and their songs can be very long...and loud!

Please visit my website for links to pictures and more resources

A Song for Swinging

Try playing this on a keyboard - even a toy one should work!

Sing a hap-py song while you swing a-long.

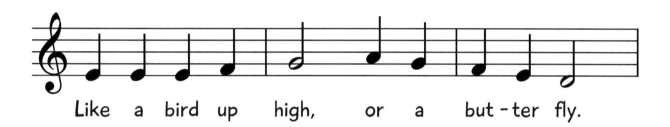

Like a bird up high, or a but-ter fly.

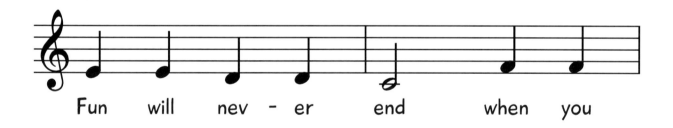

Fun will nev - er end when you

have a friend who sings a hap - py song.

CPSIA information can be obtained
at www.ICGtesting.com
Printed in the USA
LVIC06u1932091117
555671LV00003B/10